For Dee

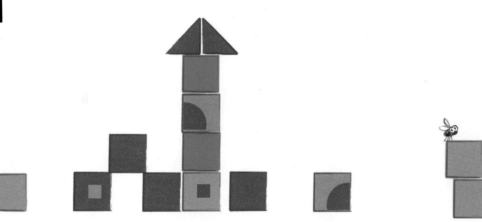

www.alisonmurray.net

**ORCHARD BOOKS**
338 Euston Road, London NW1 3BH
*Orchard Books Australia*
Level 17/207 Kent Street, Sydney, NSW 2000

First published in 2014 by Orchard Books

ISBN 978 1 40831 306 0

Text and illustrations © Alison Murray 2014

The right of Alison Murray to be identified as the author and illustrator
of this work has been asserted by her in accordance with the
Copyrights, Designs and Patents Act, 1988.

2 4 6 8 10 9 7 5 3 1

A CIP catalogue record for this book is available from the British Library.

Printed in China

Orchard Books is a division of Hachette Children's Books, an Hachette UK company.
www.hachette.co.uk

# The House That ZAC BUILT

## Alison Murray

ORCHARD

# This is the house that Zac built.

*Shoo!*

And this is the fly that
**BUZZED** on by
over the house
that Zac built.

This is the cat
that stalked the fly
that **BUZZED** on by
over the house that Zac built.

This is the cream way up high,

approached by the cat . . .

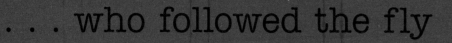

. . . who followed the fly

that BUZZED on by
over the house that Zac built.

This is the dog, deep in a dream . . .

...till

# DOWN

came the jug

and SPLASH went the cream . . . .

. . . spilt by the cat
with her head held high,
who was still determined
to catch that fly . . .

. . . which

BUZZED on by
over the house
that Zac built.

These are the lambs, calm and serene . . .

Then along came the dog,
all covered in cream . . .

who raced through the farm
when roused from his dream,

. . . ignored by the cat,
who despite all that

kept her eye on the fly
as it BUZZED on by . . .

and
STOPPED . . .

on the house
that Zac built.

Zac looked around
and gasped in alarm
when he saw the MESS
they had made on the farm!

But Zac was smart,
he knew what to do.

He patted the dog who
was trusty and true.

He collected more cream
from Daisy and then . . .

. . . he herded the lambs back into their pen.

With the cat in his arms
and the farm like new . . .

. . . he took a deep breath

and BLEW!

Off buzzed the fly,
'Meow' went the cat,
'Woof' went the dog,
and down they all sat

and gazed amazed
at the house
that Zac built.